you • Do not fear for He is with you • When I'm not here He is with you • I couldn't love you more. No, I couldn't love you more. But somebody does Jesus • Rest your eyes He is with you • I pray you find He is with you • When I let go He is with you • And I can know that He is with you • I couldn't love you more. No, I couldn't love you more. But somebody does Jesus • You are mine for a moment but His forever His • In this life I am holding you but in His arms you live • I couldn't love you more. No, I couldn't love you more • Oh, but somebody does Jesus • In the night He is with you • At morning light He is with you • Do not fear for He is with you • When I'm not here

He is with you · I couldn't love you more.
No, I couldn't love you more. But somebody
does Jesus · Rest your eyes He is with you
· I pray you find He is with you · When I let
go He is with you · And I can know that He
is with you · I couldn't love you more. No, I
couldn't love you more. But somebody does
Jesus · You are _____ for a moment but you
are His forever _____ife I am holding
you but in His a_____ve · I couldn't
love you more. No, _____t love you more
· Oh, but somebody does Jesus · In the night
He is with you · At morning light He is with
you · Do not fear for He is with you · When
I'm not here He is with you · I couldn't love
you more. No, I couldn't love you more. But

I Couldn't LOVE You More

written by
JASON INGRAM & MATT HAMMITT
lead singer of Sanctus Real

illustrated by
POLONA LOVŠIN

Tyndale House Publishers, Inc., Carol Stream, Illinois

MATT HAMMITT is the lead singer and a founding member of the band Sanctus Real. Over the past decade, the Grammy-nominated, Dove Award–winning group has released five albums and has topped the Christian radio charts with fourteen number-one and top-five radio hits.

In 2010, Matt and his wife, Sarah, found out they were expecting their third child. Already the parents of two young daughters, Emmerson and Claire, they were looking forward to an ultrasound that would reveal whether they were having a boy or a girl. "We found out it was a boy, and we were all celebrating," Matt recalls. "But only a few minutes later the doctor came in and told us that things weren't right, that half of the baby's heart wasn't developed. At that time, they didn't think he would survive."

Diagnosed with hypoplastic left heart syndrome, little Bowen, whose name means "small, victorious one," defied the odds and survived. But it hasn't been an easy road for Matt and his family. Following Bowen's birth, Matt and Sarah watched their newborn son endure two open-heart surgeries, and they spent more than three months by his bedside at C. S. Mott Children's Hospital in Ann Arbor, Michigan.

Matt and Sarah have shared the pain, as well as the joy, of their journey with others through their blog, Bowensheart.com, which has received more than one million hits to date. Sarah says, "God clearly has His hand in all of this. Our family has been called to walk through this, and we will do our best, even though it's going to be really rough at times."

"Everything I've watched happen in the hospital—all the pain I've felt—is deepening my faith, strengthening my marriage, and molding my character," Matt says. "Out of what appeared to be a well of emptiness has flowed a fountain of purpose."

Matt's album *Every Falling Tear*, released in 2011, was born out of the heart of a father wrestling with his pain but buoyed by his faith and his love for his family. "I Couldn't Love You More," one of the songs on the album, expresses a parent's desire to share Christ's unconditional love with his child.

A portion of the proceeds from both Matt's album and this book will be given to support the Whole Hearts Foundation, a 501(c)(3) nonprofit organization founded by the Hammitts that is dedicated to helping families with children suffering from congenital heart defects. Matt says, "We've met so many families like us whose children are suffering, and they are looking for hope. It has become our mission to help them find it."

POLONA LOVŠIN was born in Ljubljana, Slovenia. As a child, she spent most of her time in a small village on a farm with her grandparents. She loved playing with cats, chickens, and other farm animals.

Having always had a passion for drawing, Polona studied at a fine arts academy in Ljubljana. She has exhibited her work all around the world, in places including Italy, Slovakia, Japan, Iran, and Argentina.

When asked what inspires her work, Polona says, "I will never grow up. I'm just a little girl doing what makes me happy, whatever fulfills my curiosity."

She lives in Slovenia with her two wonderful daughters.

JASON INGRAM'S résumé reflects the diverse accomplishments of a songwriter, producer, and artist. His father, Chip Ingram, is a prominent speaker and author. Sharing the same passion for communication, Jason chose music as the vehicle for his message.

Jason has received multiple Dove Awards, including Song of the Year and Producer of the Year, as well as being named *Billboard* magazine's Christian Songwriter of the Year for both 2009 and 2010. He is also a four-time recipient of SESAC's Christian Songwriter of the Year honor. Jason had the privilege of cowriting "I Couldn't Love You More" and many other songs with Matt Hammitt.

In the night
He is with you

At morning light
He is with you

Do not fear
For He is with you

When I'm not here
He is with you

I couldn't love you more
No, I couldn't love you more

But somebody does
Jesus

Rest your eyes
He is with you

I pray you find
He is with you

When I let go
He is with you

And I can know
That He is with you

I couldn't love you more
No, I couldn't love you more

But somebody does
Jesus

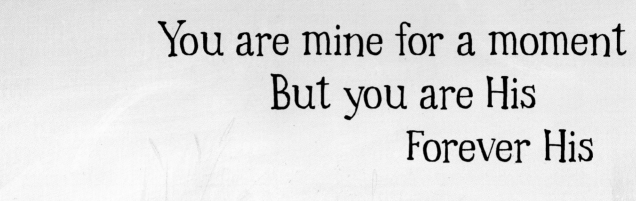

You are mine for a moment
But you are His
Forever His

In this life
I am holding you
But in His arms
you live

I couldn't love you more
No, I couldn't love you more

Oh, but somebody does
Jesus

Visit Tyndale's website for kids at www.tyndale.com/kids.

Visit Whole Hearts Foundation's website at www.bowensheart.com.

TYNDALE is a registered trademark of Tyndale House Publishers, Inc. The Tyndale Kids logo is a trademark of Tyndale House Publishers, Inc.

I Couldn't Love You More

Designed by Jacqueline L. Nuñez

Edited by Stephanie Rische

For manufacturing information regarding this product, please call 1-800-323-9400.

ISBN 978-1-4143-6739-2

Printed in China

18	17	16	15	14	13	12
7	6	5	4	3	2	1

somebody does Jesus • Rest your eyes He is with you • I pray you find He is with you • When I let go He is with you • And I can know that He is with you • I couldn't love you more. No, I couldn't love you more. But somebody does Jesus • You are mine for a moment but you are his forever His • In this life I am holding you but in His arms you live • I couldn't love you more. No, I couldn't love you Oh, but somebody does Jesus • In the night He is with you • At morning light He is with you • Do not fear for He is with you • When I'm not here He is with you • I couldn't love you more. No, I couldn't love you more. But somebody does Jesus • Rest your eyes He is with you

• I pray you find He is with you • When I let go He is with you • And I can know that He is with you • I couldn't love you more. No, I couldn't love you more. But somebody does Jesus • You are mine for a moment but you are His forever his • In this me I am holding you but in His a   u live • I couldn't love you more   t love you more • Oh, but some   sus   n the night He is with you • A   g ight He is with you • Do not fear for He is with you • When I'm not here He is wi ou • I couldn't love you more. No, I couldn't love you more. But somebody does Jesus • Rest your eyes He is with you • I pray you find He is with you • When I let go He is with you • And I can